The Hopes and Dreams Series
Jewish-Americans

Old Ways
New Ways

A story based on history

Second Edition

Tana Reiff

Illustrations by Tyler Stiene

PRO LINGUA ASSOCIATES

Pro Lingua Associates, Publishers

74 Cotton Mill Hill, Suite A315
Brattleboro, Vermont 05301 USA
Office: 802 257 7779
Orders: 800 366 4775
E-mail: orders@ProLinguaAssociates.com
SAN: 216-0579
Webstore: www.ProLinguaAssociates.com

Copyright © 2018 by Tana Reiff

Text ISBN 13: 978-0-86647-447-4 – Audio CD ISBN 13: 978-0-86647-448-1

The first edition of this book was originally published by Fearon Education, a
division of David S. Lake Publishers, Belmont, California, Copyright © 1989, later
by Pearson Education. This, the second edition, has been revised and redesigned.

The cover and illustrations are by Tyler Stiene. The book was set and designed by
Tana Reiff, consulting with A.A. Burrows, using the Adobe *Century Schoolbook*
typeface for the text. This is a digital adaptation of one of the most popular faces
of the twentieth century. Century's distinctive roman and italic fonts and its clear,
dark strokes and serifs were designed, as the name suggests, to make schoolbooks
easy to read. The display font used on the cover and titles is a 21st-century digital
invention titled Telugu. It is designed to work on all digital platforms and with Indic
scripts. Telugu is named for the Telugu people in southern India and their widely
spoken language. This is a simple, strong, and interesting sans serif display font.

This book was printed and bound by KC Book Manufacturing in North Kansas City,
Missouri. Printed in the United States. Second edition 2018

The Hopes and Dreams Series
by Tana Reiff

The Magic Paper (Mexican-Americans)
For Gold and Blood (Chinese-Americans)
Nobody Knows (African-Americans)
Little Italy (Italian-Americans)
Hungry No More (Irish-Americans)
Sent Away (Japanese-Americans)
Two Hearts (Greek-Americans)
A Different Home (Cuban-Americans)
The Family from Vietnam (Vietnamese-Americans)
Old Ways, New Ways (Jewish-Americans)

Contents

1 The Cobbler 1

2 Old Country 6

3 Friday 11

4 Mr. Fine......................15

5 Not Jewish Enough 18

6 Emma's Play 24

7 The Red Hat............... 30

8 Young People............... 35

9 A Step Too Far........... 40

10 The Theater 46

11 Family Ties 51

12 Father and Son 56

13 Freedom of Religion.... 62

Glossary 69

1 The Cobbler

New York City, Lower East Side
1914

Pound! Pound! Pound!
Solomon Gold
pounded the nail
into the shoe.
His young son Sidney
watched him work.
This was his father.
The shoemaker.
The cobbler
from another place.
A cobbler
like his father
before him.

"When does school
start up again?"
Sol asked his son.

"Next week,"
said Sidney.

"That's good,"
said Sol,
not looking up
from his work.
"School is important.
Very important.
My father
put sugar on my books.
'Learning is sweet,'
he would say.
I want you
to get good grades.
You are smart.
You work hard,
you'll do fine.
Hand me that shoe,
will you?"

Sidney handed his father
the shoe.
"How can you do this
day after day?"
the boy asked.

"What do you mean?"
asked Sol.

"This is my work.
I work hard.
I am good at what I do.
I put food
on the table.
Someday, my boy,
you'll work too."

"Not here,"
Sidney said to himself.

"You and I,
we will work
side by side,"
Sol went on.
"We will build
the business together.
Look how far
I have come already!
When I first came
to America,
I worked in a crowded shop.
I helped to make shoes
for pennies.
Now I have
my own shop."

Sidney looked
around the little room.
Maybe this was
his father's dream.
But Sidney
could never spend
his whole life here.
Helping his father
when school was out
was one thing.
But work here always?
Never!

"You are only 14,"
said Sol.
"You do not understand
how it was
for your mother and me.
You do not understand
where we come from."

"I know
you come from Europe,"
said Sidney.
"You don't speak
much English.
And you fix shoes."

"School is very good,"
laughed Sol.
"But it does not teach
some important things
you should know.
Let me tell you
how it was."

2 The Old Country

Russia, 1882

Young Solomon Gold
was sleeping.
"Wake up!"
cried his mother
in the middle
of the night.
"The house
is on fire!"

Young Sol
jumped out of bed.
He felt
a wall of heat
moving toward him.
He saw orange flashes.
He ran outside.

Sol heard
his father's voice.
"Stop it!"
cried Sol's father.

Men with sticks
were beating him.
Some of the men
threw stones.

Sol ran
to his father.
"Stop hurting my father!"
he yelled at the men.
Then Sol himself
felt stones
hit his body.
He cried out
in pain.

Two large men
pushed the boy away.
Then they all left.

Sol's father
lay in the street.
He was not dead.
But there was blood
all around him.
Sol helped him
stand up.

Over the next weeks,
Solomon Gold's father
began to feel better.
But he was angry.
"What is going on?"
he cried to Sol's mother.
"First they tell us Jews
that we are not
real Russians.
Then they pass laws.
The new laws say
Jews may not buy land.
And only a few Jews
may go to school.
Then these men come here
to beat and to kill.
They burn our house.
Now they tell us
that all Jews
must move to the city?"

"Oh, no!"
said Sol's mother.
"Our families
have lived here
for hundreds of years!
We never made
any trouble."

Even so,
the family
had to leave their home.
They went to a city
in the west of Russia.
All the Jews
had to live
in one part of the city.
It was known as
the ghetto.
Most jobs
were not open to them.

"We have taken
enough!"
said Sol's father one day.
"We cannot live
like this.
It is too hard
to be Jewish
in this country.
We must leave.
Yes! we will go to America.
The land of hopes and dreams!"

3 Friday

"So now you know,
my boy," said Sol.
"And your mother's story
is much like mine.
This is the life
we came from."

Sidney Gold
had heard the story before.

"I am happy
to work hard,"
said Sol.
"Why?
Because here,
we can be Jewish.
No one tells us
we cannot be Jewish.
And here,
you and your sister
can go to school."

Just then
two of Sol's friends
came into the shop.
Sol looked up
at the clock
on the wall.

"Is it noon already?"
he asked.

"We are early,"
said one of the men.
We came to visit
for a few minutes."

Sol's friends
came to the shop
every day.
But today was Friday.
On Fridays
all the shops
closed early.
It was Shabbat.
All the Jewish men
went to pray and sing.

"Are you coming along?"
Sol asked Sidney.

"Of course,"
said Sidney as he
locked the back door
and closed the windows.

Sol pounded in
the last nail.
He pulled off
his leather apron
as he stood up.
"Let's go!"
he said.

They walked out
into the street.
Earlier this morning
the street
was full of people.
Men sold
food and clothes
on the street.
The street was loud
and full of life.
Now the last wagon
was rolling away.

The women
were already busy inside.
Sidney's mother, Hannah,
was cooking special food
for the Friday night dinner.

Sidney turned the sign
on the door.
CLOSED, it read.
But everyone around
knew that already.
It was Friday
on the Lower East Side.
It was not a time
to do business.

4 Mr. Fine

The Gold family
lived in four rooms.
There was a tiny kitchen
with a table and chairs.
Sol and Hannah
slept in the living room.
They slept
on folding beds.
Emma, Sidney's older sister,
had a small room
off the kitchen.
Sidney shared his room
with a boarder.

The boarder
was not a member
of the family.
He lived
with the Golds
for a dollar a week.
Having a boarder
helped the Golds
make ends meet.

Each boarder
stayed about a year.
Then another one
would move in.
This week
a boarder
had moved out.

New York was crowded.
Everyone needed
a place to live.
Hannah had no trouble
finding someone
to share Sidney's room.
When Sol and Sidney
got home,
a new person was there.

"Meet our new boarder,
said Hannah.
"This is Mr. Fine.
He is a teacher."

Sol and Sidney
shook Mr. Fine's hand.
"Glad to meet you,"
they said to each other.

Sidney liked Mr. Fine
right away.
But Sol was not so sure
about this young man.
He did not like
Mr. Fine's looks.
This young man
was Jewish.
But he was
a different kind of Jew.
He acted
more like an American.
He spoke perfect English.
And why
had he not been
at temple today?

But to Sidney,
Mr. Fine seemed
very interesting.
Sidney wanted
to get to know him better.

5 Not Jewish Enough

Mr. Fine
was an English teacher.
He spent
most of his time
at the school.
But many nights
he and Sidney
sat up late together.
Mr. Fine told Sidney
about great books.
They read together.
They talked
about what they read.

Mr. Fine
did not act
like the Jews
Sidney knew.
He did not pray
three times a day.

He worked
Friday afternoons.
Friday nights,
he went
to a coffeehouse.
There, he and his friends
talked about new ideas.
He often came home
very late.

"I think
you spend too much time
with Mr. Fine,"
said Sol.
"You should spend
more time
at the temple."

"I think Mr. Fine
is very interesting,"
said Sidney.
"I want to know
all about him."

"One day,
Sol, Hannah, and Emma
were out shopping.

Sidney began
to ask Mr. Fine
some questions.

"My father
has a beard,"
said Sidney.
"Why don't you?
Aren't you Jewish?"

"I am Jewish,
Mr. Fine explained.
"I am a new kind of Jew.
We do not believe
in all the old ways."

"Do you eat kosher*?"
Sidney asked.

"Not always,"
said Mr. Fine.
"Have you ever eaten anything
that isn't kosher?"

"No," said Sidney.
"I may not do that."

"Would you like
to try some?"
asked Mr. Fine.
"It won't hurt you!"

Sidney said yes.
Then he and Mr. Fine
went to a store.
They bought food.
Much of it
was new to Sidney.
They came back
from the store
and cooked
in Hannah's kitchen.
They sat down
and enjoyed their meal.

Just then,
Hannah walked in.
What are you eating?"
she asked.

Sidney told her.
She became very angry.

"Pig meat?
Shellfish?"
Hannah yelled.
"This is not
Jewish food!
You have made
my home unclean!
Mr. Fine,
you must leave!
You put bad ideas
into our boy's head.
My husband and I
will not put up with this!"

Then Sol walked in.
When he saw
what was going on,
he became angry too.

"Go now!"
he shouted at Mr. Fine.
"Do not come back!
And do not ever
talk to my boy again!"

Mr. Fine stood up.
He picked up
a few things
from the other room.
Then he walked out
without a word.

"But Mother,"
Sidney began.
"Mr. Fine is …"

"Not a word from you!"
said Hannah.
"Now go and wash!"

"That does it!"
said Sol.
"No more boarders!"

6 Emma's Play

"You have grown up
so fast!"
said Hannah.
She smiled
at her children.
Emma was 19 now.
Sidney was 17.
"You are so beautiful,
both of you!"

Sidney
had almost finished
high school.
After school
he fixed shoes
with his father.
At night
he went
to Jewish school.
He was learning
the Jewish books.

Pretty Emma Gold
acted in Jewish plays.
The actors
spoke in Yiddish,
not in English.
Emma was the lead actor
in tonight's play.
Her family
would be right there
to watch her.

"I must go now,"
said Emma.
"The lights go down
in two hours.
I can't be late
for makeup.
And don't you
be late either!
I'll be looking
for all of three of you
from the stage!"

After the play,
Hannah, Sol, and Sidney
went to see Emma.

"How did you like the play?"
Emma asked.

"It was very fine,"
said Sidney.
"It made me think."

"You were beautiful,"
said Hannah.

Sol said nothing.
He turned away.

"How about you, Papa?"
Emma asked.
"What did you think
of the play?"

"It wasn't funny,"
said Sol.
"I thought
Yiddish plays
were funny."

"Some are funny,
said Emma.
"But this play
is about real life,"
she said.

"Is that fun,
acting out real life?"
asked Sol.

"Yes, in a way,"
said Emma.
"But I have plans.
I want to act
in English, too."

Soon after that,
Emma landed
a big part
in an English play.
The play
was going to open
on a Friday night.
The theater
was on Broadway.

"You will come and see me,
won't you?"
asked Emma.

"We cannot come
on a Friday night!"
said Sol.
"You know that.
You should not
be there either.
Not on a Friday!
It is Shabbat!
Friday is the beginning
of our day of rest.
And you know that,
young lady!"

"But this is New York,"
said Emma.
"New York
does not stop
on Friday night!"

"You want
to be rich and famous?
Fine for you!"
said Sol.
"But remember,
you are Jewish first.
Jews stop everything
on Friday nights.

Friday night
is not the time
to get rich and famous!
I, for one,
will not come to see you
if you act in a play
on a Friday!"

But Emma
went on acting
on Friday nights.
Most other nights, too.
But Sol didn't go
on any night.
He said
he couldn't understand
what they were saying.
And so Emma's father
never went
to another play.

7 The Red Hat

Sol began making shoes,
not just fixing them.
He made fine shoes.
He sold them
out of his shop.

"My shoes
are too good
for this part of the city,"
Sol told Sidney.
"I am going uptown.
I will sell my shoes
to a big uptown store.
I will get
fifty cents a pair!
Just watch me!"

So Sol
tied together
15 pairs of shoes
by their strings.
He hung

the string of shoes
around his neck.
He put on
a funny red hat.

"You are going uptown
looking like that?"
laughed Sidney.

"Yes, I am!"
said Sol.
And out the door
he went.

Sidney put his hands
over his eyes.
He shook his head.
"My father!"
he said to himself.
"People will think
he is crazy.
They will never
buy his shoes."

Sol walked
30 blocks uptown.
People looked at him.
He kept on walking.
At last,
he reached
a big store.
A Jewish family
owned the business.

"I make fine shoes,"
he told them.
"I think
your store
should sell my shoes.
Look at the toes.
Nice and round.
Look at the bottoms.
Look inside them.
Have you ever seen
such nice shoes?
And smell them!
Smell that beautiful leather!
I'll sell you
my handmade shoes
for seventy-five cents a pair!"

"You are dreaming!"
said the man in charge.
"I'll give you twenty-five cents."

"Sixty-five,"
said Sol.

"Forty,"
said the man.

"I say sixty cents a pair
and no less,"
said Sol.

"Fifty cents
and that's it,"
said the man.

"OK, fifty cents
a pair,"
said Sol.

"And I'll give you
ten cents
for that silly red hat!"
added the man.

"The hat
is not for sale!"
said Sol.
"People will know me
by my hat!"

　　Sure enough,
Sol walked home
with no shoes
around his neck.
And sure enough,
people got to know him.
The big stores
always knew
when Solomon Gold
was coming.
They could spot
that silly red hat
a block away.

8 Young People

Sidney Gold
became a student
at City College.
It was free.
His father
wanted him to go.
He still lived
with his parents.
As often as he could,
he worked in the shoe shop.

One summer morning
Sidney asked his father
if they could talk.

"I want you
to understand something,"
Sidney began.
"I plan to finish college.
But I do not plan
to come back here.
I cannot look at shoes
all my life."

"I do understand,"
said Sol.
"You are a bright boy.
Your whole life
is in front of you.
You must do
big things!
But I have
an idea, my boy.
We could build
this business.
Together, you and me."

"You already have
two other people
working for you,"
"You make and sell
lots of shoes."

"We should
start a factory,"
said Sol.
"We could make shoes
by the hundreds.
You can learn
how to run the business.

"I am not sure
I want to be in business,"
said Sidney.
"I am not sure
what I want to be.
But I will think about it."

It was Friday.
Almost noon.
Sol began
to close up the shop.

"I'll go
to the temple
with you,"
said Sidney.
"But I have plans
for tonight.
I'm going out."

"To see your sister
in some Broadway play?"
Sol asked.

"No, not that,"
said Sidney.
"I'm going
to meet friends
at a coffeehouse.
We are going to
get together
and talk there."

"What is wrong
with you young people?"
Sol shouted.
"You are so smart.
But you don't care
about Jewish life.
Today is Friday!
This is not the time
for plays and coffee!"

But Sidney
went to the coffeehouse.
It was a dark room,
filled with people
and smoke.
Sidney lit his pipe.

       Sometimes
there was music.
Sometimes people
read poetry
or parts of books
they were writing.
Sidney and the others
talked about
important things
late into the night.
They even talked
about Emma's new play.

Sidney enjoyed
this kind of talk.
He enjoyed it very much,
but he did not want
to face his father
when he got home.
The other young people
had the same problem.

9 A Step Too Far

College life
was new and different.
So many bright people.
So many new ideas.
Sidney loved it all.

Two years
went by quickly.
Now it was time
to think about
his father's business idea.
So Sidney signed up
for a business course.

He also took
a writing course.
On the first day of class,
Sidney had a surprise.
The professor
walked into the room.

It was Mr. Fine!
Sidney had not seen him
for years.
Not since
he was a boarder
at the Golds' house.
Not since Sol
had told Mr. Fine
to leave.

   "I'm so happy
to see you,"
said Mr. Fine to Sidney.
"How are you doing?"

   Sidney told him
about the business course.

   "That's very good,"
said Mr. Fine.
"I am sure
you will do well
in business."

Sidney did do well
in the business course.
He came away
with many ideas.

"I have been thinking,"
Sidney told his father.
"Let's start our factory
when I finish school.
We will make
the best shoes.
And we will make
more of them
than anyone else!"

"That's my boy!"
said Sol.
"Hard work
and long hours
make dreams come true
in America!"

But Sidney
also enjoyed
the writing course.
He did not tell Sol
who the professor was.

But he spent many hours
writing papers
for Mr. Fine's class.
He learned
a lot about writing.
He also learned
that he loved to write.

"You are a good writer,"
Mr. Fine told Sidney.
"You should think about
writing for a living."

"Not me,"
said Sidney.
"My father and I
plan to start
a shoe factory."

"Is this
what you want to do
with your life?"
Mr. Fine asked.

"Of course,"
said Sidney.

"Will you follow
the old ways
of being a Jew?"
Mr. Fine asked.

"I don't think so,"
said Sidney.
"I stopped going to temple
about a year ago.
Do you still meet
with your friends?"

"Yes, I do,"
said Mr. Fine.
"Now, I don't want
to get you into trouble.
But you are welcome
to come along with me."

"I'd like that,"
said Sidney.

The next Monday
a woman
came into the shoe shop.
"I saw your son
at the library,"
she said.

"He was with that man.
Your last boarder."

Sol asked Sidney about it
that night.

"No, Papa,"
said Sidney.
"I was not
with Mr. Fine."

"You lie to me!"
said Sol.
"I won't have it!
I told that man
to never talk to you again!
First you start going
to the coffeehouse
on Friday nights.
Then you stop coming
to the temple with me.
And now you lie to me!
That is enough!
Find yourself
another place to live!
You are not my son!"

10 The Theater

Sidney found
a little room
to live in
near City College.
He also found
a part-time job
in an office.
He needed money
to pay the rent.
He didn't work
for his father anymore.

But Sidney
kept on taking
business courses.
He kept thinking
things would get better
with Sol.
Someday he and his father
would start their factory.
But time went on
and he never heard
from his father.

Sidney still saw
Mr. Fine,
at the college
and after class.
His friend and teacher
helped him
with his writing.
More than anything,
Sidney enjoyed writing.

One day
he met his sister
for dinner.

"How's Papa?"
he asked Emma.

"He is starting
a shoe factory,"
Emma told Sidney.
"He says
that he must do it
by himself.
He says
he has no son."

"The factory
should be on the East Side,"
said Sidney.
"That way,
it will be close
to the river.
The ships.
The docks.
He can ship shoes
out of New York."

"I'll tell him,"
laughed Emma.

Then Sidney
pulled out
a thick pile of paper.
"I wrote a play,"
he said.
"It's about a woman
who lost touch
with her parents.
Will you read it?"

"Sure," said Emma.
"Is there a part for me
to play?"

"You are the star
of the play," said Sidney.

Emma laughed.

"I mean it!"
said Sidney.
"I want you
for the lead part!"

"May I take this
to read at home?"
asked Emma,
holding the play.

In a few days
Emma and Sidney
got together again.

"It's a great play!"
Emma said.
"I showed it
to the man
who runs the theater.
He likes your play.
He wants to stage it."

"You're kidding!"
said Sidney.

But what Emma said
was true.
The theater
signed up the play
for its fall season.

Sidney came
to see the actors
work on the play.

"Who is
that pretty woman
with brown hair?"
he asked Emma.

"That's Helen Little,"
Emma told him.
"She works
for the theater,
in the business office.
Do you want
to meet her?
She's not Jewish."

"I'd love to meet her,"
Sidney said.

11 Family Ties

Sidney and Helen
liked each other
the minute they met.
It was love
at first sight.

Sidney's play
opened that fall.
He and Helen
went out together
every night
after the play.

Sol never came
to see the play.
The play
his son wrote.
The play
his daughter acted in.
Sol never saw it.

Sidney went out
to dinner with Emma
once a week.
He wanted
to see his sister,
but he also cared
about his parents,
and he wanted
to hear about them.

Sol put his factory
in a building
on the East Side
near the river.

"How's the shoe business?"
Sidney asked Emma
one night at dinner.

"Papa knows
how to make shoes,"
Emma began slowly.
"And he knows
how to sell them.
But he doesn't have
enough time
to do both."

"Tell him
to hire sales people,"
said Sidney.
"He has things set up.
Now other people
can do the sales work."

That's how it went
week after week.
Sidney would give ideas
to Emma.
She would carry them
back to Sol.
Sol would do
just what Sidney said.

Emma took home
other news, too.
Sidney and Helen
were going to marry!
Sol and Hannah
were not happy.
Helen was not Jewish.
This made Sol
even more angry
with Sidney.

Emma and Hannah
went to the wedding.
Sol did not go.

After the wedding
Helen came to dinners
with Emma and Sidney.
The three of them
became best friends.
They always had
a good time together.
Like Sidney,
Helen had good ideas
for Sol's shoe business.
Emma still carried the
ideas
to Sol.
He used those ideas,
and his business grew.

But one night at dinner
Emma looked very sad.
Her eyes
were red.
She had been crying.

"I have
very bad news,"
said Emma.
"Papa is not well.
The doctor says
he does not have
long to live."

"I must see him,"
said Sidney.
"I cannot
let him die
without talking to him."

Emma told their parents
what Sidney had said.

"I don't have a son,"
said Sol.

"Oh, come now,"
Hannah said.
"You have a son.
And he wants very much
to see his father."

12 Father and Son

Sidney tapped
on the door.
"It's me,"
he said.
"Please let me in."

His mother
opened the door.
She put her arms
around Sidney.

"Your father
is in the back room,"
she whispered.

Sidney walked
into the room.
"Papa?" he said softly.

Sol looked up
from his bed.

"Has my son
come home?"
he asked.
He sounded
a little mixed up.

"I have come
to see you,"
said Sidney.
"I am married now.
I live with my wife.
Her name is Helen."

"Have you changed
your ways?"
Sol asked.

"Please, Papa,"
said Sidney.
There were tears
in his eyes.
It was hard
to speak.
"Please don't be angry.
I have not gone back
to the old ways
of being Jewish.

But that doesn't make me
a bad person."

"You and I,
we built
our shoe factory,"
said Sol.

Sidney started
to talk.
Sol broke in.

"You know
this is true,"
Sol went on.
"You went to school
and learned
all about business.
You told Emma
your good ideas.
I listened
to everything
you told her."

"I guess
you are right,"
said Sidney.
"We built the business
together."

"Come here, my son,"
said Sol.

Sidney sat down
on the bed
near his father.

"I hope
you can forgive me."
said Sol.
"I always loved you.
But my pride
made me treat you
the way I did.
I am sorry."

Sidney had never heard
Sol say he was sorry
about anything.
Ever. Not in his whole life.

He remembered
his father saying,
"Never say you're sorry.
Just do things right
the first time."

Sidney reached out
and held Sol's hand.
"I love you, Papa,"
he whispered.

"What will happen
when I die?"
Sol asked.
His voice cracked
as he spoke.
"Who will carry on?"

"I will,
if you want me to,"
said Sidney.
"I will take care
of the business."

Sol's mouth
turned to a smile.

"In one way or another
my dream
will come true,"
he said.
"The business
will be yours."

Sol closed his eyes,
and he never woke up.

13 Freedom of Religion

Sidney took over
the shoe business.
He was surprised
at how much
he enjoyed
running the factory.
At last,
he could put to use
all his good ideas.

Sidney and Helen
made the business
grow very large.
They made
lots of money.
They bought
a big house
on Long Island.
They had three children.
They asked Hannah
to move in with them.
The children
called her Bubbe.

Emma married
the man who ran the theater.
They lived
in the city.
But they often visited
the house on Long Island.

One day,
Sidney said to Helen,
"We don't have
enough time together.
Let's go away
for the weekend.
Just the two of us.
Bubbe can watch
the children."

So Sidney and Helen
drove up the coast.
They stopped
at a big hotel
by the ocean.

Sidney went inside.
He waited
at the front desk.
The man behind the desk
was reading a book.

Sidney rang the bell
on the desk.
"I have been waiting,"
he called to the man.
"May I please
book a room?"

The man
turned around.
"We have no rooms left,"
he said to Sidney.

"What do you mean?
asked Sidney.
"I saw you give a key
to that other family.
You'll have to give me
a better reason."

"The reason
is who you are,"
said the man.

"Jewish, you mean?"
cried Sidney.

"Let me tell you something.
My grandfather
came to America
for freedom of religion.
My father
worked his fingers
to the bone
in this country.
I run a big shoe factory
in New York
that he started.
I have the right
to stay anywhere
I want to!"

"Your kind of people
are not welcome here,"
said the man.
And he went back
to his book.

Sidney could not believe
what was happening.
This man was telling him
that America
was not a free country
for Jews?

Sidney grew angry.
America was not
the old country.
Jews should be as free
as any other Americans!

Then and there
Sidney made up his mind.
He would work
for the rights of Jews.
He would write and talk
and raise money.
He would tell
other Americans
to be fair to Jews.

Sidney walked
back to the car.

"I just learned something
about myself,"
he told Helen.
"I am Jewish.
I *really* am Jewish."

"You knew that,
said Helen.

"But maybe
I never understood it,"
said Sidney.
"I can't be
like my father.
I can't be
that kind of Jew.
But my blood is Jewish.
Nothing will ever
change that.
And I don't want to change.
I am proud of the people
I come from.
I learned a lot
from my parents.
And Mr. Fine
showed me how
to be Jewish
in today's world.
From all of this,
I became Sidney Gold —
a Jew,
an American,
a person.
I must be free
to be all three."

Glossary

Definitions and examples of certain words and terms used in the story

---

Chapter 1 — Happy New Year page 1

cobbler — A person who makes or repairs shoes.
The cobbler from another place.

pound (to pound) — To hit something hard.
nail — A sharp piece of metal used to connect two
things together.
Solomon Gold pounded the nail into the shoe.

spend — To use time (or money).
*But Sidney could never spend his whole
life here.*

(school) was out — Not open, finished at the end of
the school day.
Helping his father when school was out …

Chapter 2 — The Old Country   <small>page 6</small>

flashes — Sudden and bright light, like lightning.
   He saw orange flashes.

beating (to beat) — To hit something or someone
   very hard many times.
   Men with sticks were beating him.

yelled (to yell) — To speak very loudly; to shout.
   "Stop hurting my father," he yelled at
   the men.

even so — However.
   Even so, the family had to leave their home.

ghetto — A part of a city where a special group of
   people live, separate from the main city.
   It (the part of the city) was known as
   the ghetto.

Chapter 3 — Friday page 11

Shabbat — The Jewish holy day of rest.
... all the shops closed early. It was Shabbat.

pulled off (to pull off) — To remove a piece of clothing.

apron — A piece of cloth or leather worn across a person's front for protection.
He pulled off his apron as he stood up.

Lower East Side — A part of New York City where immigrant groups, especially Jews, lived. It is now more fashionable.
It was Friday on the Lower East Side.

Chapter 4 — Mr. Fine page 15

folding bed — A small bed (may also called "cot")
that can be folded and easily stored.
They slept on folding beds.

shared (to share) — To use, or have something
together.
Sidney shared his room with a boarder.

boarder — A person who pays to have a room and
sometimes meals with the owner of a house.
Sidney shared his room with a boarder.

(to) make ends meet — To earn enough money to
pay the bills.
*Having a boarder helped the Golds make
ends meet.*

move in/out — To begin living (move in) in a place
and end living there (move out).
*Then another one would move in. This week a
boarder had moved out.*

temple — A holy Jewish house for worship and prayer.
And why had he not been at temple today?

Chapter 5 — Not Jewish Enough   page 18

act (to act) — Here, it means he did not seem to be Jewish in his actions.
   Mr. Fine did not act like the Jews he knew.

beard — Hair on men's face.
   "My father has a beard," said Sydney.

kosher — Foods that are allowed and prepared by Jewish law.
   "Do you eat kosher?" Sydney asked.

pig meat/shellfish — Food that is not allowed by Jewish law.
   "Pig met? Shellfish?" Hannah yelled.

unclean — Not kosher.
   "You have made my home unclean!"

(to) put up with — To accept or allow certain behavior.
   My husband and I will not put up with this!

Chapter 6 — Emma's Play page 24

grown up (to grow up) — To become older, from
 childhood to adulthood.
 "You have grown up so fast!"

acted (to act) — To have a part in a play.
 Pretty Emma Gold acted in Jewish plays.

actors — The people who act in a play.
 The actors spoke in Yiddish, not in English.

Yiddish — A language based on German, with words
 from Hebrew and other languages. It is spoken in
 the United States, Israel, and Russia.
 The actors spoke in Yiddish, not in English.

lead actor — The most important actor.
 Emma was the lead actor in tonight's play.

the lights go down — The lights in the playhouse are
 lowered to show the play is beginning.
 "The lights go down in two hours ...

makeup — Colors and lines put on the actors' faces.
 I can't be late for makeup.

stage — The place where the actors act.
*I'll be looking for all three of you from
the stage.*

part — In a play, one of the characters.

landed (to land) — To get something one has
been "fishing for."
Emma landed a big part.

Broadway — The most famous theater area of
New York. Also the street name.
The theater was on Broadway.

Chapter 7 — The Red Hat   page 30

uptown — The northern or upper part of New York
City, where there are many big stores.
"I am going uptown ...

(to) put on —Here, placing a hat on one's head in
order to wear it.

funny — Strange, unusual, laughable.
He put on a funny red hat.

dreaming (to dream) — Here, it means that
    one's thinking is not realistic; not possible.
in charge — having responsibility for making
    decisions.
    "You are dreaming!" said the man in charge.

spot (to spot) — See or notice.

silly — Laughable. Something that is not fashionable.
    They could spot that silly red hat.

Chapter 8 — Young People   page 35

run (to run) — To operate or manage a business.
    You can learn how to run a business.

lit (to light) — To use fire to make something burn.

pipe — A small bowl with a tube coming out of it for
    smoking tobacco.
    Sydney lit his pipe.

face (to face) — To meet or see someone or
    something that may be unpleasant.
    He did not want to face his father ...

Chapter 9 — A Step Too Far   page 40

(to) get you into trouble — To do something
  that gives another person a problem.
  I don't want to get you in trouble.

Chapter 10 — The Theater   page 46

docks — The place where ships come to load or unload.
ship (to ship) — To send goods away by ship. Nowadays,
  also to send by truck, airplane, or any other way.
  *Close to the river ... The docks ... He can ship
  shoes out of New York.*

pulled out (to pull out) — To take out or remove
  something from someplace.
pile — Many things on top of each other.
  Then Sydney pulled out a thick pile of paper.

lost touch (to lose touch) — To no longer have contact
  with someone or something.
  *It's about a woman who lost touch with her
  parents.*

stage (to stage) — To prepare and show a play for the public.
> *"He likes your play. He wants to stage it."*

kidding — Joking; not really serious.
> *"You're kidding," said Sydney.*

sign up (to sign up) — To agree to show or do something.
> *The theater signed up the play for the fall season.*

Chapter 11 — Family Ties   page 51

the minute they met — Immediately.
> *Sidney and Helen liked each other the minute they met.*

went out (to go out) — To go places together as friends.
> *He and Helen went out together every night after the play.*

hire (to hire) — To give a job to someone.
> *Tell him to hire sales people.*

best friends — Very close friends who like each other and do many things together.
> *The three of them were best friends.*

Chapter 12 — Father and Son   page 56

whispered (to whisper) — To speak very softly and quietly.
"Your father is in the back room," she whispered.

mixed up — Confused; not clear-minded.
He sounded a little mixed up.

broke (to break in) — To interrupt a conversation.
Sidney started to say something. Sol broke in.

forgive (to forgive) — To let an unpleasant happening be forgotten and no longer important.
"I hope you can forgive me."

pride — One's feeling that one is right and does not need to apologize or change.
But my pride made me treat you the way I did.

cracked (to crack) — To break or change suddenly.
His voice cracked as he spoke.

(to) carry on — To continue some work or plan.
"Who will carry on?"

Chapter 13 — Freedom of Religion   page62

took over (to take over) —- To take control of
some activity.
Sidney took over the shoe business.

Bubbe — (BUB-ee) is Yiddish for grandmother.
The children called her Bubbe.

front desk — The place in a hotel where one
registers for a room.
He waited at the front desk.

book (to book) — To make a reservation for a
room or travel.
"May I please book a room?"

worked his fingers to the bone — Worked
very, very hard and long.
*My father worked his fingers to the bone
in this country.*

(to) raise money — To work for a cause (such as
human rights) by getting people to give
money to support the cause.
He would write and talk and raise money.